Aud ||||||||||||||| :
D1235274
Power Pieces for Kids and Teens
Revised Edition

A collection of fun comedic and powerful
dramatic one-minute monologues designed
for ages 5 to 18.

By Deborah Maddox

A must have for amateur and professional actors alike.

Website:
www.AuditionMonologues.com
Email Address:
Questions@AuditionMonologues.com

Audition Monologues: Power Pieces for Kids and Teens
Revised Edition
Copyright 2011/Deborah Maddox
All rights reserved

ISBN # 978-0-9716827-3-3

Published by:
Lucid Solutions
P.O. Box 32141
Mesa, Arizona 85275-2141

www.AuditionMonologues.com

Book Description...

This book has it all! Audition Tested, Industry Approved! **Audition Monologues: Power Pieces for Kids and Teens** is an excellent collection of fun comedic and powerful dramatic monologues designed for children between the ages of 5 and 18. Expressively written in a way to enable the actor to project emotional range effectively and to experience the situation of the character firsthand. The content is entertaining, includes surprising twists, and is appealing to both professional and amateur actors. Industry professionals such as casting directors, agents, acting coaches and actors have highly praised this book and actively recommend it to their students, colleagues and peers. Often casting decisions are made within one minute's time, therefore, a two to four minute monologue can be lengthy and inappropriate. **Audition Monologues: Power Pieces for Kids and Teens** offers effective monologues with unlimited character choices. In this book you will also find valuable audition tips written from a Talent Agent's point of view.

A message from the author;

To the young people of today and of tomorrow, help pave the way to global peace and harmony for all humanity. Erase the hate and set an example of strength and acceptance. Surround yourself with people who believe in you and walk away from the ones who do not. You really do have the power to influence others.

This book is dedicated to my family, friends and industry colleagues whom have been so invaluable and supportive. Thank you for your direction and insight. Your time and expertise has significantly helped my dream become a reality and I am eternally grateful.

I give a special thank you to my husband Mike for his support and to Scott for his support and contribution to the cover.

Finally, I thank my daughter, Sidney, for she has been an inspiration to my work. I was truly blessed the day she was born.

May you pursue your dreams and make them a reality.

Table of Contents

Table of Contents Continued...

How To Pick The Right Material

The material an actor chooses for the audition is essential. This choice can make or break the outcome. Considering the fact that the audition process tends to go quickly, a two to four minute monologue can be too long and inappropriate. *In fact, casting decisions are often made within one minute's time.* Most often, the determination of whether or not the actor possesses strong acting skills is made within the first thirty seconds of delivery. During the next thirty seconds, the decision is made whether or not to add the actor to the callback list.

Give the industry professionals what they want to see: *A one-minute power piece.* **Audition Monologues: Power Pieces for Kids and Teens** provides fun comedic monologues and empowering drama monologues, which enables the actor to be creative with his/her own character development and versatility. When performed, the monologues are delivered from a first person point of view, enabling the actor to project emotional range and to experience the situation of the character firsthand. These monologues are written in a style that allows the actor to readily identify with the character and play out the scenario effectively. This book is a perfect source for beginner and professional actors alike.

Acting is a wonderful way to express creativity and talent. Remember that there are no two people on this earth who are the same. Therefore, when you audition, give of yourself. Find confidence in knowing that your delivery is unique. If you have the passion within yourself to perform, it will be recognized and, eventually, be appreciated by others.

I hope you enjoy performing these monologues as much as I have enjoyed writing them. Relax, focus and become the character. May you keep them to the edge of their seats.

How To Prepare For An Audition

For amateur and experienced actors alike, the *audition* is a significant part of acting. Although the nature of each audition may be different, the etiquette consistently remains the same. Whether the audition is for a role in film, television, theater or simply for agency representation, the audition is a systematic process in which industry professionals make final casting decisions. Industry professionals may consist of casting directors, producers, directors or agency representatives.

The Audition: Excitement, anticipation, anxiety, confidence. These are just a few emotions an actor may experience during an audition because final decisions are made through this process. Along with strong acting skills, it is imperative to possess strong auditioning skills. How you present yourself and the impression that is made will greatly affect the outcome of the audition.

The following are valuable guidelines that every actor should consider for an audition. Being seen as suitable for a part ultimately lies in the hands of the industry professionals. However, there are ways of beating the odds. For example, producers, directors and writers always have an idea of what they are looking for. Have you heard the phrase, "I'll know it when I see it?" The purpose of the audition is for the industry professionals to find the actor that they have visualized for the part. Before you go to an audition, be clear on what they are seeking. Often you will be informed of appropriate wardrobe for the part. If wardrobe requirements have not been stated, then dress the part. If the character is non-descript, then simply wear colors that bring out your eyes and look best with your hair color. Wear little or no jewelry. You want the focus to be on you and your delivery, not your shiny bracelet or trendy outfit. Young children should not wear makeup. Teenage girls should keep their makeup looking clean, fresh and natural. Be prepared to be flexible, and if given the chance, show that you can portray a variety of character types and emotional range.

Professionalism: Professionalism is the foundation of strong audition etiquette. The entertainment industry is a business, just like any other profession. It should never be looked at as a playground for egos. During the audition process, industry professionals are not only looking for acting ability, they are also considering whether or not the actors will be easy to work with, that the know what they are doing, and can take direction well.

When you enter an audition room, enter with confidence and a smile. Introduce yourself and stand at your mark. If you are asked any questions or if you are asked to tell a little about yourself, offer full and complete sentences. Yes and no answers are rarely effective. And remember that the interviewers are people, just like you. If you find your nerves starting to escalate, you may want to try to visualize everyone in the room in their pajamas. That may help you to see things on the lighter side. But ultimately, by staying focused on your character, you will find that the people in the room will disappear.

The goal is to leave a memorable impression without over-extending your welcome. Listen to direction, take your mark and give it your best shot. If you make a mistake, continue on. They are not looking for perfection, just strong delivery and effective characterization. Never ask to start over. If they want to see you do it again, they will make that request. If you are performing a monologue, only state the name of the piece. Generally they are not interested in the full story line because time is of importance. When *slating* your name, take advantage of those few seconds to let your personality shine. Remember, you can tell a lot about a person just by their "hello."

Characterization: Whether you are performing a monologue, dialogue or a commercial script read, getting into character is key. Give great thought to the character's persona. Create and visualize the character in your mind. Decide what kind of personality you will give the character. What about their demeanor? Maybe the character has a sense of humor or is soft-spoken or condescending. Maybe he/she is strong-willed or quirky, over confident or insecure. Perhaps the character has a nervous twitch. Be deliberate with the body language you choose for the character. One of the greatest things about being an actor is that what you offer is completely up to you. Regardless of the specifics you choose to implement, be creative and find confidence in your choices.

Reaction: A large part of acting is reacting. When you perform a *monologue* at an audition, there are no props or acting partners to respond to. Therefore, it is up to you to create and visualize the stage and circumstances within your own mind, then effectively perform it so that the industry professionals visualize the same thing you are projecting. Take a moment and think about the art of pantomime. The mime communicates everything through facial expression and body language. Generally, it is not effective for actors to pretend to pick up a phone or take a sip of tea from an invisible teacup. However, like the mime, it is very effective for actors to communicate through facial expression and body language.

Many actors forget this factor while performing monologues. They tend to get so involved with their how they are going to say the words, that they dismiss the relationship with their acting partner or prop, invisible or otherwise. Think and feel during the delivery of each line. Become your character. Take your time. Respond to your invisible prop or partner. Become your character and have fun with it. Remember, there is no right way, just your way.

Comedy

Changes
Comedy
Child/Teen Female

There is a big transition from little girl to young woman. Maybe a few manners classes can help.

My mom says becoming a woman starts early in life. About my age she says. Now, all of a sudden, everything becomes important, especially my appearance. The other day, mom bought me Vanilla Mist perfume, Red Raspberry lipstick and Chestnut colored highlights for my hair. I felt like a food! Mom also says it's real important how you act at the dinner table. Well, can *you* hold in a burp? I can't. If I try to hold one in, I get heartburn. I guess she thought I needed serious help, so she sent me to manners class. On the first day of class I asked the instructor, "Hey, what do you do if you can't hold in a burp?" To sum it up, you are supposed to say, "excuse me." I also learned that you shouldn't talk with your mouth full. OK.....then when are you supposed to say something? What's the point of having dinner together if you can't talk to each other? Really...this becoming a woman stuff is ridiculous.

Notes:_____

_____

_____

Being Little Isn't Easy
Comedy
Child Male/Female

Kids perceive things differently than adults do. Being a kid has it's advantages and disadvantages.

Being a little kid has its advantages and disadvantages. Let's talk about grown-ups for a minute. Do they think kids can't hear or something? It happens to me all of the time. They lean down and get real close to your face and ask how old you are or what your name is. And they talk real loud, too. Hello! I can hear...thank you! The other day I was at the toy store with my mom and this lady came up to me. She had really big red hair and big pink lips. She kneeled down and told me how cute I was, pinching both of my cheeks. Look, I already know I'm cute and don't pinch my cheeks. The worst part was that her breath smelled like my dog Lefty's breath...right after he eats his dog food. YUK!

Notes:_____

_____

_____

Dating Again
Comedy
Female Teen

Feeling slightly helpless, she watches her mother enter the dating world. Maybe mom isn't thinking clearly. At this point, she must put it in fate's hands.

It has been absolutely crazy since my mom decided to start dating again. She seems to have dates all the time... and not always with the same guy. She says she needs to be "open to what is out there." I say, "Hey, if he's cute, go for it." My mom signed up with a dating service. She asked me if I thought she was being desperate. I said, "Of course not," nodding my head yes. You should see some of these guys. First of all, my mom thinks she has an age range of about fifteen years. I have seen everything from Mr. College Grad to Mr. Executive. I think her worst looking date was Stan. He stood no taller than five feet, and his nose was almost as tall as he was. One night as my mom was leaving, I said, "Hey Mom, you may need a booster chair for this one." She didn't find that very funny. The worst part is that she likes Stan. The next time he came to pick her up, he was wearing platform shoes. I guess he heard me. Oops!

Notes:_____

_____

_____

Distant Admiration
Comedy
Teen Male

He has admired her since he was ten years old. He finally decides to go for it.

Oh look, there she is. Wow. She is just so....don't you think she's awesome? And she gets better every year. Come on, let's go over and sit by her. Come on. What do you mean? No, I'm not crazy. So, I didn't letter in football. So what! So, I'm not the most popular guy in school, but hey, I've got potential. Just look at her. OK, OK, so her boyfriend used me as a punching bag last year. What's your point? It's been a whole year. I've been working out. He probably won't even recognize me. Besides, the only reason why he used me as a punching bag in the first place was because I accidentally tripped, and my spaghetti went flying onto his face. Now that was a Kodak moment! Yeah, yeah, I know... so was my face. Alright, Alright. Keep laughing and I may use you as my own punching bag.

Notes:_____

_____

_____

Humiliation
Comedy
Child/Teen Female

Is there a way to turn back time? She has just been kissed by the school nerd!

Lindsay, you are never going to believe this. My life is over! Jeremy came up to me at lunch today and gave me one big smack-a-roo...right on the lips! In front of everybody! I couldn't believe it. He drives my crazy. Rumor has it, he picks his nose in English class...Yuk. Last week during CPR class, he tried to kiss Annie, the dummy! Instead of doing what you are supposed to do and say, "Annie, Annie, are you all right?" He said, "Annie, Annie, you're all right." I have brushed my teeth four times since I got home. I even gargled with peroxide! Now everybody thinks I like him. Well, maybe. I guess he is kinda cute...Ok maybe just a little.

Notes:_____

_____

_____

The Warning
Comedy
Child Male/Female

Lexie just moved into the neighborhood. Her new friend immediately informs her about the bully on the block.

Lexie, you moved into the neighborhood just in the nick of time. You need to know about creepy Rudy. He lives next door and he loves to torture and make fun of other kids. Last month he dumped a bucket of live earth worms down Daisy Mae's pants. She hasn't walked the same since. Just last week he emptied a coffee can full of crickets into his own sister's bed, while she was sleeping. Poor Sarah, she still twitches. I've heard rumors that my friend Destiny is next. My inside sources say that he has caught fifteen frogs and is storing them in his basement. The way I see it? It's our turn to torture Rudy. Are you in? Great! My uncle has a straight jacket that I'm sure I can borrow without him knowing. Tonight when the clock strikes midnight, Sarah will let us in the backdoor. We will hold Rudy down, put the straight jacket on him and stick a few daddy long leg spiders down his shirt. How many? Oh, I don't know. Twenty-five sounds like a good number. Let him feel those creepy crawlers for a couple hours. He'll never bother anybody again.

Notes:_____

_____

_____

Chester
Comedy
Child/Teen Male/Female

This is his/her idea of how to handle a dirty cat.

I begged my mom for a whole year before she let me get my cat, Chester. Mom always reminds me of how much responsibility animals are. "You have to feed them and play with them everyday", she would say. Well, she finally gave in. See, my cat Chester isn't like other cats. He is always getting dirty. I finally got tired of sleeping with a dirty cat. How do you bathe a cat you ask? You can't just put him in the bathtub with a rubber ducky. So, I've come up with the best way. Step number one, open the toilet lid. Step two; add one ½ bottle of shampoo, Johnson's No More Tear's is the best. Step three; place cat in toilet and close lid fast, so that the cat doesn't get out. Sit on the lid if you have to, then flush the toilet. And wallah! A perfectly clean cat. By the way, have you seen Chester? It's time for his bath. He always seems to hide when it's bath time. Chester!!!!!

Notes:_____

_____

_____

Grandma Harriett's Meatloaf
Comedy
Child/Teen Male/Female

Grandma's World Famous Meatloaf should be renamed to Grandma's Famous Moving Meatloaf.

Grandmas house? Tonight? For dinner? What is she making? Her world famous meatloaf? Oh, no. Mom, I am surprised that you survived your childhood. I have to break it to you. Grandma's meatloaf, yeah, the one she calls world famous? Well, it's not so world famous. Last time I stayed over at their house, I was helping her make meatloaf. She asked me to get the oatmeal out of the cupboard. As I watched her put the ingredients in the bowl, I noticed the oatmeal was moving. Uh, yeah. It had a bunch of tiny little bugs moving around in it. I said, "Grandma, look!!!" And all she said was, "Don't tell your Grandpa. He doesn't need to know." Mom, you probably grew up eating bugs and you didn't even know it....hahahaha! Don't get me wrong. I love Grandma, but tonight, I'll be taking my own TV dinner, thank you very much. Actually, I'm taking two. The other one is for poor Grandpa. He could use a good meal.

Notes:_____
_____
_____

Chick Magnet
Comedy
Child/Teen Male

He seems to have a few secrets up his sleeves and decides to share with his friends.

Did you know that I can get any girl to like me? I am a true chick magnet. Just look at me. Oh, hey there. Did you just see how she looked at me? See, they can't get enough. I've got the muscles, the personality....I've got it all. The babes line up. What's my secret? It's all about how you present yourself. First, tell her that you made brownies for your family the night before and that you saved her one. I always keep a brownie in my pocket for emergencies. You never know who you are going to run into. Then watch her melt in your hands. They love a guy who can cook. And don't forget the walk. You can walk like a nerd, like this (imitate a walk) or you can be cool, like this (imitate a walk). Sweet. But do you really want to know want they want? Ok, I'll tell you. What really does it for the babes...is my aftershave. No, I don't shave. You're missing the point. Brut...Walgreen's...Two bucks. The other day, Sarah told me I smelled like her grandfather. Trust me, it's a sure thing.

Notes:_____

_____

_____

Infatuation
Comedy
Teen Female

Be careful what you ask for. You just might get it.

I had been watching him for months. I'd watch him at football practice and every time he would say Hi, my heart would just start pounding. Well, of course the minute Lisa introduced us, he asked me out to a party. It all started when he asked me to dance. I started to groove and well, he started to move. Thankful wasn't the word when that song ended. So I suggested we go get something to eat. Anything to get off the dance floor. I do have a reputation to uphold you know. I guess it was the cherry tomato that did it for me. I knew the minute he stuck it in his mouth. Do you know how extremely difficult it is to clean little tomato seeds out of your hair? Ah, very. It was like, so embarrassing. Anyway, I dumped him. So, know any cute guys?

Notes:_____

_____

_____

Lets Play
Comedy
Child Female

She is convinced that younger brothers are so much more fun to play with than older brothers.

My younger brother Charlie is so much fun to play with. He always does whatever I tell him to do. He will play with me all day long and complain very little. My older brother Andy likes to pick on me all the time. He never does anything I tell him to do. I never can figure that out. He really doesn't know what he is missing. Yesterday, we went skateboarding. I wore my yellow dress and Charlie wore my pink dress. When we passed Andy and his friends, I thought to myself, that Andy sure doesn't know what he is missing.

Notes:_____

_____

_____

Peer Pressure
Comedy
Teen Female

She reassures her friend of a future to be part of the "in-crowd" and become more popular.

All right, let's think for a minute. Oh, I've got it! All you need is some networking and a little P.R. What better way to become more popular than to throw a party? Oh, come on. It will be fun. Think about it. How often is it when your parent's leave for the whole weekend? Better yet, you don't have to go with them. OK, you should have the party this Saturday night, and then you'll have all day Sunday to pick up the mess. You have always wondered if David likes you. Well, here's your chance. And you know how Jennifer loves parties. She'll become your friend instantly. Oh and be sure to tell her that her boyfriend is not your type. Then she won't feel threatened. Oh yeah, and don't forget to compliment her every thirty minutes...and be sure to laugh at all of her jokes. This is your only chance. Oh my gosh. What are we going to wear?

Notes:_____

_____

_____

120 Degrees
Comedy
Child/Teen Male/Female

There are many ways to get out of going to school. This way may not be so fool proof.

Last week I woke up with a sore throat. It was Wednesday and I thought, yes! If you add up the weekend, that's five, count them, five days of no school. So I got up, looked in the mirror, put on my suffering face, then presented myself to my mom. That morning, she seemed to be especially sympathetic. I thought to myself, I actually might pull this off. This time, she was putty in my hands. So, she brought me some hot tea and said that if had a temperature I could stay home from school. Ahhhhh, that was sweet music to my ears. Play Station here I come! As she walked away, an amazing idea flashed through my head, kinda like an insurance policy. Ok, uh, note to self; never and I mean never, put a thermometer under the lampshade while the light is on. At that moment, I saw the putty in my hands, that being my mom, look at me with this, *I better be ready to leave in 10 minutes* look. I guess 120 degrees was a little too high of a temperature and off to school I went. But hey, I really did have a sore throat.

Notes:_____

_____

_____

The Girlfriend
Comedy
Child/Teen Male/Female

He/she is not real happy with dad's new girlfriend.

I knew when my mom and dad got a divorce, they would have new people in their lives. I just never thought that it would be like this. Leona. Just her name makes me want to puke. The first time I met her, she came to our house for dinner. I knew there was trouble when she knew exactly where to find the coffee cups. As she brought the cups out, she looked at me with this look like...*it's just a matter of time sweetie.* Then I looked over at dad. Usually by this time you would find him on the couch, feet propped up, watching T.V. Instead, he is making conversation and laughing at Leona's stupid jokes. You should hear how she laughs (imitate an obnoxious laugh). What does he see in her? Mom is so much better. The only good thing about all of this is that Leona has a four-year-old rug rat named Hanna. I'll be able to handle the rug rat just fine. She has the words, *personal slave*, written all over her forehead.

Notes:_____

_____

_____

College Bound
Comedy
Teen Female

Feeling extremely confident, she decides to take her mother on regarding her future. After all, she feels she is old enough to make her own decisions.

Oh, Mom, you think you know everything. You don't always know what's best for me. I know what's best for me and right now, I know that I don't want to go to college. What's the point? I'm working at the Piggly Wiggly, making my own money. I pay my car payments. Besides, I don't even know what I want to study. Really Mom, you need to learn to live in the *now*. And *now* is what matters. I'll worry about my future later, like…in the future. What? Move out? By this weekend? Oh, come on Mom, that's pretty lame. You're serious, aren't you. OK, OK, you win. I'll go. I'll go to college. Well, when you put it that way, nursing school doesn't look so bad after all.

Notes:_____

_____

_____

One Bad Apple
Comedy
Child/Teen Female

A funeral brings family together. Unfortunately, you can pick your friends, but you can't pick your family members.

I went to my very first funeral over the weekend. I didn't want to go but my mom made me go. She said I had to go to pay my respects, whatever that means. I didn't even know her. OK, I respect ya, Great Aunt Edna, even though I didn't know ya. *Whatever.* On the way there, all my mom talked about was how her Aunt Edna was always so feisty, "Never took any lip from anybody." When we got to the funeral home, a lot of family was there, and….so was Lenny. Lenny is my very *distant*, third cousin and every time he sees me, he winks at me. Sure enough, he came right up to me and asked if I would like to meet him in Parlor A. He said he had already scoped out the room and there was nobody in there except for some old guy's dead body. Gross! My mom says that I should mellow about it, that his hormones are just a little out of control. Personally, I think he's pretty creepy. I can't believe I have to be related to him.

Notes:_____
_____
_____

His Only Chance
Comedy
Teen Male

At some point in our lives, we just have to go for it. In this case, he wishes he never did.

There she is. Our eyes have met but I can't get up my nerve. Wow, she is amazing. Total perfection. Tall, long blonde hair, with big blue eyes that are screaming out to me. Jason! Jason! Ja...... Well, it's not everyday I get attention like this. If I don't go up to her right now, I will never have another chance. Just do it. Yeah, like the NIKE commercials. JUST DO IT! Ok, here I go. Uh, Hi. I noticed you have been looking over at me and I thought I would come over to introduce myself. My name is Ja....Huh? You noticed what? My fly is open? Oh, it sure is. Uh, thanks. Well, uh, you girls have a great day. Walk away Jason, just turn around and walk away. Don't look back, just keep walking.

Notes:_____

_____

_____

Be Good to Your Pet
Comedy
Child Female

He/she loves to play with the family dog. But this family pet has no say.

My dog Rusty is my best friend. He follows me everywhere I go. We have so much in common. We like to eat cookies and we both want to be on the Rug Rats show when we grow up. But, we are still working on his tricks. When I tell him to sit, he lays down. He sure can be lazy. Every morning after we watch T.V., we go upstairs to play house. Rusty looks so cute when I dress him up in my purple pajamas. Except my hair clips seem to pinch his ears, so he doesn't wear those for very long. Sometimes he gives me sad eyes, but I think he is just pretending that he is tired. You should always give your dog lots of playtime and rest. Just like little kids like me, if you play all day, you will sleep all night.

Notes:_____

_____

_____

Pink or Red
Comedy
Child/Teen Female

She is ready to be different than the other girls...or is she?

Really? I mean really? Jessica....hello!!! This is not the time to sign up for Average Joe School of Boring. Do you really think you are going to get Ryan's attention by dressing like Amanda and Stephanie all of the time? They wear the same pink shoes laces every week. Jess, Jess, Jess, Jess, Jess. In this world, there are leaders and there are followers. There are bosses and there are employees. There are Great Danes and there are Toy Poodles. Would you rather be a Madagascar cockroach or just a plan old regular cockroach? No, I'm not calling you a cockroach. It's just an example. Please, stay focused. Don't you see, if we keep going to school dressing like everybody else, we just end up, well, like everybody else. Come on. Just repeat after me. I...am ready...to make a change...to take a stand...to show them that I am a leader...to show them that I am not afraid to have my own style. Are you with me? Excellent!!! Ok. Now, it's time to get creative. To-morrow, let's...Oh, I know...let's wear our *red* shoe laces instead of our pink ones. Brilliant. Sometimes I just amaze myself.

Notes:_____

_____

Drama

The Bully
Drama
Child/Teen Male/Female

After many months of torment, he/she finally gets the courage to confront his/her biggest fear, then triumphs.

Don't you have anything better to do? Just leave me alone. What...you think because you are bigger than I am that you have the right to push me around? Or is it the fact that you want to show these other kids here how tough you are? Well, I'm tired of you. Today it ends. No more! I am telling you right now, no more putting ketchup in my hair. No more tripping me in the halls. No more grabbing my books. NO MORE! What is it that you want? Do you want to punch me? Do you want to give me a black eye? What is it? Because today, I'm going to give it right back to you. Today, it ends. Right here. Well...Hello?...What...All talk and no action? I should have figured.

Notes:_____

_____

_____

The New Kid
Drama
Child/Teen Female

Moving to a new place and making new friends is not easy.

My mom says, "Enjoy life now. Being a kid can be the best years of your life." Sorry, but I don't get it. The best years? I don't think so. This year has been so hard. It all started when daddy got fired from his job. I have never seen my parents yell and scream at each other so much. When daddy left, we moved here to Tulsa. The only thing that has been good is that I met you. It seems like you are the only one that has been nice to me. Yesterday, Tiffany Applegate said she wanted to walk home with me. She told me to meet her at the flagpole after school. I waited there for twenty minutes until Mr. Blackwell came over to me and said I better get on home. Half way home, I saw Tiffany and her friends peeking around a wall...laughing at me. Yeah right...the best years of my life. Why do they have to be so mean? It's not easy being the new kid in town. I miss my friends back home in Indiana, but I'm glad I have you.

Notes:_____

_____

_____

The Rush
Drama
Teen Male

The time he had with his friend was really great. But was it worth it?

Sometimes, the days got so boring. Especially, around here. This town isn't that big. Everyday was the same old thing. School, homework, go to bed. School, homework, go to bed. I lived for the weekends. It seemed to be the only time I felt free. Free of my parents...free of my responsibilities. Me and my buddy, Josh, were always looking for things to do. But you can skip so many rocks across the lake or throw toilet paper on just so many trees. Last summer we started to hang around the railroad. It was pretty cool to watch the trains pull in. The best part was when they would go straight through the station without slowing down. That's when we got brave. Who could stand the closest to a passing train without moving? I used to love to close my eyes and feel the vibrations as the train passed. The sound of the engine was so powerful that my heart would pound right out of my chest. It was such a rush. Today, I have nightmares about those vibrations and sounds. That's how I lost my buddy, Josh.

Notes:_____

_____

_____

7:30
Drama
Teen Female

This teenage girl travels the country in hopes that she can make a difference.

Hi, my name is Paula Gardner. I am here today to talk to you about texting and driving. Last year my friend Rebecca was driving us to soccer practice. We were on a highway going the speed limit, which was about 45 miles per hour. The last thing I remember was Rebecca saying to me that she forgot to text our friend Katie and tell her what time to meet us later that night. The next thing I knew, I woke up in the hospital, confused and unable to feel my legs. Rebecca had lost control of the car while she was sending a text to Katie. She died on the scene. As you can see, I am in a wheel chair and I am now paralyzed. It's hard to think about how a simple text, 7:30, something so short, ended up taking the life of such a great girl, and how that text has changed my life forever. I didn't want to feel trapped in this chair, so I decided to try and make a difference. I now visit schools across the country to simply say; Do not text and drive. Hopefully you will remember me for the rest of your life and that you will learn from my story. Make the choice to be safe. Thank you.

Notes:_____

_____

_____

Son and Father
Drama
Teen Male (age range 17-18)

He loves his father, but he also realizes it is time to take a stand and try to live his own life.

Don't you realize that the pressures I have from school are nowhere near the pressures you put on me? I can't take it anymore, Dad. I have tried to live up to your expectations. I have tried to make you proud. But...I don't want to join the military. Why won't you let me make some of my own choices? I'll be 18 soon and everybody keeps telling me that I have my whole life ahead of me. But whose life is it? Yours or mine? I look at all of your medals of honor and I respect what you have done, Dad. I really do. I just have different interests than you do. Please let me go to Juilliard. Music is a huge part of me. I want to study it, and I want to play it, and maybe someday, I'll be able to make money doing it. I know you don't think that could happen, but you have to let me try. I'll never know if I don't try. Please Dad. Please let me do what I love to do and be who I am...because I can't walk in your shoes. I can't be you.

Notes:_____

_____

_____

Audition Monologues: Power Pieces for Kids and Teens

Mistaken Identity
Drama
Child/Teen Male

He is a patient at a home for the mentally challenged. He thinks he wants a baseball glove for his birthday.

Next week is my birthday. I am going to be one year older than I was last year. One whole year. I want a baseball glove for my birthday. Gary has one. Last year I wanted a baseball glove too, but nobody gave me one. All I want is a baseball glove...just one...baseball glove. Every year I ask for a baseball glove and every year I don't get one. I keep asking and asking and asking, but I don't get one. Gary has one. Why does Gary have a baseball glove, and I don't? They just don't listen to me. All they care about is your medicine. "Gary, take your medicine, it will make you feel better." That's all I hear. "It's time for your medicine." "Here Gary, take your medicine...take your medicine!" Yesterday, I told Nurse Harrington that if the medicine was so good, she should take it. Funny, huh? I told her I want a baseball glove...just one. Gary has one. All she cares about is the medicine. Everyday...time for medicine. All I care about is a baseball glove...I wish she would stop calling me Gary.

Notes_____
_____
_____

Losing A Friend
Drama
Child/Teen Female

The day that her best friend is moving away has finally come. She thinks about the time they had together and deeply reflects on their friendship.

I'll never forget the day my best friend Cindy told me she was moving to Canada. I couldn't believe it, and so far away. I felt awful, especially because we had an argument the day before. Cindy is the type of friend that has always been there for me. I could tell her anything. The day I went out for cheerleading and didn't make it, Cindy was there. "Let's go to the movies," she said, "My treat." She did things like that all of the time. When my dog Max ran away, Cindy was right there with me, walking around the neighborhood for hours. And ya know? Cindy found him. And now, today is the day we have to say goodbye. This is it. I will probably never see her again. I feel like I'm losing a part of myself. I hope I have been as good of a friend to Cindy as she has been to me. I'm really going to miss her.

Notes:_____

_____

_____

Guilt
Drama
Teen Male (age range 16-18)

The death of his father has been on his shoulders for too long. Are there any magic words to help make the pain go away?

My progress? Yeah, Dr. Phillips, I know it's been a whole year. I am very aware that it has been a year. I have had to live everyday of that year, feeling the pain of missing my dad. Everyday I try to tell myself, "OK, life goes on." Just like you say Doc, "Today is today. Be happy today. I'm still alive, let go and move on." Yeah, right! Give me a break! Don't you see? My dad is gone…because of me. I should have never asked him to take me target shooting that day. I just wanted to spend some time with him. I didn't know that the gun would accidentally go off. It's not fair. All you people tell me is to forgive myself and forget. "Go on with your life Danny." But I can't! I try to get that day out of my head, but I can't! It's just not that easy. I just wanted to spend some time with him. That's all I wanted. And now, he's gone.

Notes:_____

_____

_____

Erase Hate
Drama
Teen Female

She decides to confront a fellow student whom embodies ignorance.

So here you stand, right in front of me, judging me. Who are you to judge me? Yeah we have differences, but that shouldn't be a bad thing. Don't you realize, there are no two people on this earth who are exactly the same. Nobody is the same. Why can't you appreciate our differences and see how we are alike? But you choose to close your eyes. Well, open them! You are a person. I am a person. We both go to school. We both have friends. We both have families. Whether you want to admit it or not, we both have feelings. We are two kids growing up in the same world, both of us trying to figure out how to live in this world. Look, I haven't figured it all out, but I do know who I am and what I believe. And there you stand, right in front of me, unable to look past the color of my skin.

Notes:_____

_____

_____

The Perfectionist
Drama
Male/Female Teen

When it comes to this mother, nothing is ever good enough.

Yes. OK? I admit it. I make mistakes. So does everyone else. I'm not perfect Mom. I will never be perfect, no matter how hard I try. You expect so much from me. I feel like when I mess up, my whole world is going to crumble because you are sure to remind me of how much of a failure you think I am. Did you know that when I go to the grocery store for you, I spend twenty minutes trying to pick the perfect tomatoes for you? I spend twenty minutes on your stupid tomatoes! Perfection! That's what it's all about, isn't it? Perfection. Well, I give up. I'm not perfect and I could spend hours looking for the best tomatoes. But I will never find them, will I. Will I? No, I won't. No matter what I do, no matter how hard I try, in your eyes, it will never be enough...will it.

Notes:_____

_____

_____

Not Fair
Drama
Teen Female

She finally gets the courage to tell her mom of her frustrations since her parent's divorce.

Come on Mom. Didn't you or daddy think about how your divorce was going to effect me? Why couldn't you have tried to work things out? Well, I don't think you gave it enough of a chance. I hate having to go to his place every single weekend. It's not fair. I never can do anything with my friends because I have to go visit him. I love daddy and I do want to see him, but does it have to be every weekend? On Monday, Jackson Everett asked me to go to his end of the year party. When I called daddy to see if he would take me, he said he already got us tickets to the Met's game...club seats. That's great for dad, but I would rather go to the party. Mom, you have to do something. I don't want to hurt his feelings, but I want to hang out with my friends. Why did you guys have to breakup anyway? My life is so complicated now.

Notes:_____

_____

_____

Concerned Friend
Drama
Teen Female

She is starting to realize that her friend may have an eating disorder. She decides to communicate to her mother about her own observations.

Hey Mom, can I talk to you for a minute? You know how you are always saying that Allison is too thin? I think you're right and she does have a problem. Last weekend when I spent the night at her house, she ate tons of junk and then disappeared to the bathroom for fifteen minutes. I asked her if she felt OK. She said she was fine. The other day at school, I went into the girl's bathroom a few minutes after Allison. I heard her getting sick in one of the stalls. When she came out, I asked if everything was OK, and she answered that she was fine, as if it was no big deal. We eat lunch together almost everyday, and I have noticed she always runs off to the bathroom before I finish my lunch. It seems like she doesn't want me to go with her. Mom, Allison is getting way too thin, and she is always complaining about her weight. I have tried to talk to her about it, but she says that I don't know what I am talking about. I will lose her as a friend if I say something to her mom. What do you think I should I do?

Notes:_____

_____

_____

Who Am I?
Drama
Female Teen

Finding out the news that she is adopted has her curiosity.

You are not going to believe this. My mom told me over the weekend that I am adopted. Yeah, I'm totally serious. At first I was shocked and then I was kinda mad that she didn't tell me sooner. She said she wanted to tell me when she thought I was old enough to understand. And now, it all makes sense. I've never told anyone this before, but I've always thought I was different than my family. You know, like, how they act or laugh. You have even said to me how I don't look anything like Jenna or Robbie. I always wondered where I got my blue eyes from. Now my head is spinning and all I can think about is who my real mother is and why she gave me up. I want to know what she was like, if I look like her. I just have this feeling like I need to know. My mom says that she doesn't have any details about her but she would help me find out. Then she got all teary eyed and told me she thinks that kids who are adopted, are the luckiest kids of all, because their real mothers had the courage to have them in the first place. That makes me want to know who she is even more.

Notes:_____

_____

_____

Stronger Than Cancer
Drama
Teen Male

He agrees to be interviewed for a documentary about kids fighting cancer.

How am I feeling? Not real great, but I'm hanging in there. Everyday I go through my treatments. I throw up almost everyday and loosing a little of my hair has been kind of a drag. The doctors and my parents talk about how well the treatment is working, so that is good. In the beginning, they had told my parents that I wasn't going to make it. That was four months ago. Hey, I'm still here! So, what else do you want to know? Well, I'm not just a cancer patient. I am a kid who has a life. I used to play soccer all of the time and I was the top scorer on my team. I really miss going to school and hanging out with my friends. But right now, this is my reality, and it's not fun at all. But, you know? I'm going to beat this thing. They keep telling me to stay positive and strong. This has been really been hard on my parents. I have to beat this, not just for me, but for them.

Notes:_____

_____

_____

The Foster Child
Drama
Child Male/Female

The courts say it's time to go back home. Unfortunately, home is not a safe and secure place to go. He/she desperately begs for protection.

I want to stay here. I don't want to go with them. Please don't let them take me away. I'm scared. You said we would all be together...that we were a family. You said I was like one of your own. Why can't you adopt me so I can stay here? Please, I didn't do anything wrong. This isn't fair. Please don't let them send me back to my real mother. She never changes. She always ends up hitting me. I hate her. I don't love her! I love you. How can you let them take me? I don't care what the judge says. I've been here for a whole year. I'm happy here. Do something! I can't go back to her. Please!

Notes:_____

_____

_____

The News
Drama
Teen Female

They inform her of her estranged father's unexpected death. As she starts to process the realization, she tells her friend how she is feeling.

How do I feel? To be honest, I don't know how I'm supposed to feel right now. You know, I didn't even ask how he died? Part of me wants to cry and part of me says good riddance. I remember when I was 7 years old. He took me to the zoo, just he and I. I will never forget that day, because on that day, he was just my dad. He bought me cotton candy, and he even let me ride the elephant by myself. On that day I felt only love for him. As I grew older, I started to remember the nights that he would come into my room, and I could smell his drunken breath. That's when I hated him. My skin would crawl. I learned to go somewhere else. I had this elevator in my mind that I would climb into, and it would take me directly into space and cruise through the stars. In my mind, I was as far away from him as possible. Now, he is dead. He put me through so much hurt and yet, I guess I still loved him. It's just really confusing.

Notes:_____

_____

_____

Who's Responsibility Is It?
Drama
Teen Male (age range 17-18)

He feels completely responsible once he learns a friend is in a coma.

I told him he shouldn't get into the car and drive. The party was across town, and I didn't know very many people there except for Roger. During the night, I saw him drinking. He was staggering a little, and I knew he was drunk. When it was time to leave, I told him that I would take him home. I knew he shouldn't drive. That's when he got in my face and shouted, "No way! Get out of my face! I'm fine." And he pushed me away. He said he didn't want to leave his car overnight. It's all my fault, isn't it? I should have stopped him from getting into his car. Now he's in a coma...because of me. I should have stopped him. I should have stopped him from getting into his car. Do you know if he is going to make it?

Notes:_____

_____

_____

Regret
Drama
Teen Female (age range 17-18)

She confides in her friend, hoping that she may find some answers to her problem.

Your parents tell you one thing, but then he looks into your eyes and he tells you that he loves you. What do you think I did? Follow my parent's advice or follow my heart? Yeah, I followed my heart. Big mistake! Now, he tells Lori Sayers that he loves her. I'm not ready to become a mother! Why did this have to happen to me? I feel like I'm being punished. Can you see me with a baby? I don't know how to take care of a baby. How am I supposed to finish school? How will I support it? I can't even support myself. And my parents. What do I tell them? I can see it now. My dad will say something like "You are going to have to take responsibility for your actions young lady." Then, SLAM! And the door is going to shut right in my face. I'm so scared. What am I going to do?

Notes:_____

_____

_____

Don't Leave
Drama
Child Male/Female

Mommy and daddy are not getting along. As daddy is leaving the house, she begins to beg him to stay.

What do you mean you are leaving? For how long? What do you mean for awhile? Daddy, you never leave us. Why are you leaving? No, Daddy. I don't want you to go! You need to stay here with mommy and me. We are a family. Families are supposed to be together! Please don't leave. Not now. Why do you have to leave right now? Please, Daddy, don't leave us. It's not fair. Don't go. I love you...don't go! Daddy, come back. Please come back!

Notes:_____

_____

_____

My Territory Ese'
Drama
Teen Male (age range 17-18)

Life is all too real in this neighborhood. Business is business, and this is his hood. So don't cross over the line, if you want to live.

I live here, bro. Get it straight, Amigo. This hood belonged to my grandfather, then my father and now, me. This is my domain. Here, I am King. Don't come into my territory. If you come close, I will look for you. It's all about business, Ese', and this is my place of business. Here, what I say...goes. How many times do I have to warn you? You are stepping on dangerous grounds. I have seen you and your guys cruise a little too much around here. Ombre', this is your last chance. This is my last warning. You don't get anymore chances. Don't mess with me. I hope you understand what I am saying.

Notes:_____

_____

_____

Her Mother's Footsteps
Drama
Teen Female

She likes a boy that is too old for her. She doesn't realize it now, but mother really may know what is best.

That's not fair Mom. I can't believe you are saying this. No. You can't make me stop seeing him. So what if he is three years older than I am. Daddy was 3 years older than you. What's the difference? There's no difference. Besides, Nick would never leave like daddy did. I am almost 16 years old. I can make my own decisions. You can't rule my life anymore. I won't let you. I am so tired of you telling me who I can hang around with and who I can't. All you are doing is pushing me away. Why can't you just trust me? Because you love me? You love me? No you don't. If you loved me, you would want me to be happy. You are being so unfair. You can't stop me from seeing him!!! Please!!! Don't do this. It's not fair. It's not fair.

Notes:_____

_____

_____

The Rage Inside
Drama
Teen Male

Now he has to answer to the school officials and his parents. After thinking about what he did, he wishes he could take it back.

I don't know what came over me. I guess because he was easy. I knew he wouldn't fight back. Everyone was crowding around and yelling "Kick his butt!" "Hit him!" I thought if I walked away, then everyone would think I didn't have any guts. It was something that I had to do. If I didn't do it, then I would be next. I guess I just thought that it was going to be him or me. I just kept punching him...over and over again. Finally he just lay there. He didn't even move. Then he looked at me and whispered, "Why are you doing this?" Then I realized, that this kid has never done anything to me...nothing. I wish I could take it back. How long are you going to suspend me for? A week? Are my parents on their way? They are going to be so mad at me. I know. It was a stupid thing for me to do. I'm sorry. I really am.

Notes:_____

_____

_____

En Mi Corazon
Drama
Child Male/Female

With another baby on the way, certain decisions are made that don't make sense.

We have a very large family. I have seven brothers and sisters. My dad is always working and my mom is very busy with all of us kids. My mom is expecting another baby. I was happy when I first heard the news, but last night I heard my parents crying about it. Today my mom told me that when the baby is born…it will be going away…to live with another family…a family that will be able to take care of the baby…a family not as big as ours. I couldn't believe what I was hearing. She said we can't afford to take care of it. I told her I didn't understand, and she said to me, " Mijo/Mija, mis hijos son parte de mi y nunca los dejare, en mi corazon." She said "my children will always be a part of me and I will never let them go in my heart". That's all she said. Then a tear rolled down her cheek.

Notes:_____

_____

_____

Learning the Hard Way
Drama
Teen Male

His mistake not only affected his own life, but it also affected the people that he loves. He now speaks at high schools sharing his experience.

It's been six months since I was arrested for buying drugs. That was the worst day of my life. When the undercover officer showed me his badge, my stomach went right through my throat. I was scared to death. My family said they were totally surprised to find out I even did drugs. Uncle George said I didn't look the type. He said kids like me aren't supposed to get in that kind of trouble. But it's out there. It's pretty much everywhere. You go to a party and one thing leads to another. Getting arrested was the best thing to happen to me. It saved my life. I went through an addiction program and I have been drug free ever since. But none of it was worth the pain I caused my parents. When my mom found out, she broke down and cried. I didn't mean to hurt her. I now realize I could have ruined my future and my life. I am here to tell you today, don't do drugs. Trust me, none of it was worth it. Stay strong and don't give in. In the long run, you will be glad you did.

Notes:_____

_____

_____

The Breakup
Drama
Teen Female

He is leaving for college soon, so he has decided to break up with her, thinking it might be easier now than later. She doesn't take the news well.

I can't believe you are doing this to me, here, right now. Why? Why! It makes no sense. Stop, don't even try to hold my hand right now. Ok, I know you are leaving for college soon, but, so what. Justin, we have been going out for a whole year. Doesn't any of that mean something to you? I thought we were going to be together. Why now? Prom is in four weeks. You graduate in 2 months. I don't understand. I know we have been arguing a lot lately, but. I can't believe this. What am I supposed to do now? You have no idea how much I am hurting right now. Is it...is it another girl? Justin, do you like someone else? Please tell me. Tell me the truth, because this is not what I expected when you said you wanted to talk to me. College. That's your reason. Great. Well I think that is a stupid reason and I can't believe you are doing this. I'm going home. Just leave me alone.

Notes:_____
_____
_____

I Miss My Mom
Drama
Child/Teen Male/Female

Mom is getting married and things are just not the same anymore.

My mom is getting married tomorrow. I guess it's OK. I like Jerry and everything, but...well, he's pretty nice to me, I guess. Ever since mom told me she was getting married, she doesn't spend time with me anymore. She is always telling me to go outside and play. I liked it when it was just me and my mom. She would take me to the park to play ball or we would go for ice cream or go to the movies. Now, she is always busy or spending time with Jerry. Why do I have to share my mom with somebody else anyway? We were fine the way we were.

Notes:_____

_____

_____

The Grieving Father
Drama
Teen Male/Female (age range 17-18)

His/Her father can't find it within himself to overcome his wife's death. He drinks to hide the pain and it has gotten out of hand.

You can't live like this anymore. Ever since mom died, you drink all of the time. You're an alcoholic, Dad. Can't you see that? Everyday I come home from school and find you passed out somewhere in the house. I can't even bring my friends home anymore. Just because I'm young doesn't mean I don't know what is going on. I know that's not coffee in your blue cup. My friends aren't stupid, either. When was the last time you took a shower? Dad, please. Why can't you realize...mom didn't die because of you. It wasn't your fault. Yeah, I think about her everyday too, and it still hurts, but something inside of me says to keep going and live my life. Please Dad, get some help. I don't want to lose you too.

Notes:_____

_____

_____

Military Bound
Drama
Teem Female (age range 17-18)

She has decided to join the Army. She hopes that her parents will understand her call to duty.

Mom, Dad, can I talk to you guys for a minute? There is something that I want to tell you and I am hoping that you will support me. I want to be a soldier. I have been thinking about it for a long time and today at school they had a recruiter from the Army come and speak to our class. He talked about how being in the Army is an honorable thing to do. You are part of a huge organization that has one goal in mind. To protect and serve. After listening to the Sergeant today, I have decided that I want to protect and serve our country too. They will even help with my college and I know you have been stressing on that. Dad, don't worry, of course I'm still your little princess. I'll always be your princess. It's not like you are losing me. You both have always told me how strong and tough I am. I've had to be that way, growing up with my older brothers. This will give me a chance to travel and go to different places. I'm ready to see what's out there. Mom, Dad, will you support me?

Notes:_____

_____

_____

The Boyfriend
Drama
Teen Female

Her boyfriend unexpectedly breaks up with her because he likes someone else.

Aaron broke up with me today. I can't believe it. I think he likes Angela from our 7th period math class. He seems to stare at her dimensions more than the ones on his paper. Oh Trish, it was so awful. At lunchtime I met him over at the tree by the snack bar. This morning when he told me he needed to talk to me, I thought he was going to ask me to go with him to Brittany's party this weekend. Instead, he said he wanted to break up and that maybe we should see other people for awhile. And that was it. I couldn't even get out of him, why? I am so confused. For the last four months that we have been going out, I thought things were fine. I am so upset. I really like him.

Notes:_____

_____

_____

Enough is Enough
Drama
Child/Teen Female

She confronts the friends of the school bully.

Why don't you guys just shut up! It is so easy for you and Andy to put other kids down. You think you're *all that*. Well, you're not. Why is it so hard for you to be nice? Just because she's overweight doesn't give you the right to pick on her. She has been crying everyday after school for a whole week. What if it was you or she was your sister or your cousin? How do you think you would feel? And what's up with Andy? I can't believe you are still friends with him. You guys were never like this until you became friends with him. Are you afraid that if you are not his friend, he will do the same thing to you? He's a mean jerk and I don't know why you waste your time with him. I hope someday you guys will feel like Samantha does right now. And if you took the time to get to know her, you would see she is really fun to hang out with. I hope you get a clue someday. Just leave her alone. You're being total jerks.

Notes:_____

_____

_____

Notes:

Notes:_____
_____
_____
_____
_____
_____
_____
_____
_____
_____
_____
_____
_____
_____
_____
_____
_____
_____
_____
_____
_____
_____
_____
_____

Notes:

Notes:_____
_____
_____
_____
_____
_____
_____
_____
_____
_____
_____
_____
_____
_____
_____
_____
_____
_____
_____
_____
_____
_____
_____
_____
_____
_____

Notes:

Also available:
Audition Monologues: Power Pieces for Women
Audition Monologues: Power Pieces for Men

To Order

Power Pieces For Kids and Teens   **$12.95**
Power Pieces For Women   **$14.95**
Power Pieces for Men   **$14.95**

Coming Soon...

**Monólogos para Actores: Temas Poderosos para
Niños y Adolescentes**

Add $3.00 for Shipping and Handling
Add $.50 for each additional book
To order through the **internet**:
www.AuditionMonologues.com

Customer Service: Questions@AuditionMonologues.com

To order through the **mail**:
Send check or money order along with the following order
form to:
Lucid Solutions
P.O. Box 32141
Mesa, Arizona 85275-2141

- -

Which book?_____
How many? _____ (Qty) X $_____/ea.......... = _____
Sales Tax (For Arizona residents only, add 8.95%)... = _____
Shipping/Handling ……………………………..= _____
  ($3.00 for first book, $0.50/each additional book)
                                         Total = _____
Check#:_____   Money Order #:_____
Please print the following customer billing information:
Ship my order to:

Name:_____

Address:_____

City:_____ State:_____ Zip:_____

Phone Number:_____/_____/_____

Email Address:_____

About the Author...

Deborah Maddox has over 23 years experience marketing, booking and developing actors and models on an international level. Ms. Maddox owns her own talent agency and continues to work as an Agent, helping talent achieve their goals.

**Please visit www.AuditionMonologues.com
for reviews.**

**Customer Service:
Questions@AuditionMonologues.com**

Also written by Deborah Maddox
**"Audition Monologues: Power Pieces for Women"
"Audition Monologues: Power Pieces for Men"**

Coming Soon...
"Monólogos para Actores: Temas Poderosos para Niños y Adolescentes"

I will never close another door
before I have opened it,

I will never not open a door
that stands before me,

Fear has lost it's power and
it will never prevail again,

I will live the experience,
not just dream about it.

Deborah Maddox